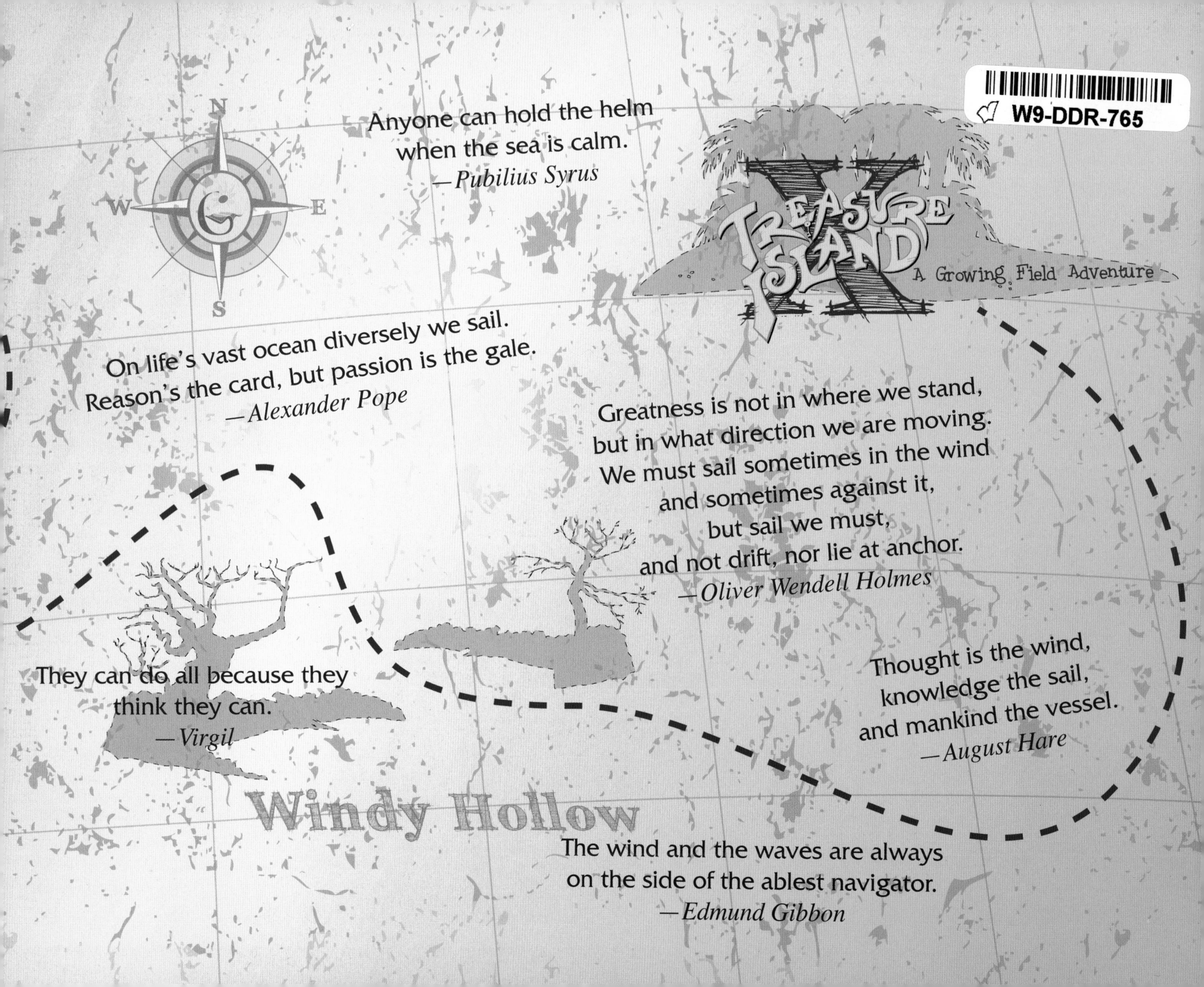

N
W
E
S
Anyone can hold the helm
when the sea is calm.
—Pubilius Syrus
W9-DDR-765
Treasure Island
A Growing Field Adventure
On life's vast ocean diversely we sail.
Reason's the card, but passion is the gale.
—Alexander Pope
Greatness is not in where we stand,
but in what direction we are moving.
We must sail sometimes in the wind
and sometimes against it,
but sail we must,
and not drift, nor lie at anchor.
—Oliver Wendell Holmes
They can do all because they
think they can.
—Virgil
Thought is the wind,
knowledge the sail,
and mankind the vessel.
—August Hare
Windy Hollow
The wind and the waves are always
on the side of the ablest navigator.
—Edmund Gibbon

The Growing Field series was inspired by, and written in memory of,
my colleague, mentor, and friend Jason Dahl –
the Captain of Flight 93 that crashed in Pennsylvania on September 11, 2001.
May your voice – and your leadership message – live on forever!

The Growing Field series is dedicated to my sister Michele.
You believed in me and this series long before I did...
with a world of love and thanks.

Treasure Island *is dedicated to my brother Michael,*
a modern day pirate who has shown me how to sail without fear
through life's challenges. I love you, Bro.

– Mark Hoog

Thanks to my teachers for their direction
during my journey to my own Treasure Island.

– Mark Wayne Adams

A portion of all Growing Field proceeds are donated to the
Children's Leadership Institute for the promotion of youth character education.
A portion of all Growing Field proceeds are donated to the Jason Dahl Scholarship Fund.

TREASURE ISLAND
A Growing Field Adventure
Written by Mark E. Hoog
Illustrated by Mark Wayne Adams
A story of responsibility.
A story of navigating life.
A story of leadership
for children of all ages.

This is a work of fiction. All names, characters, places, or incidents are the product of the author's imagination or are used fictitiously, and any resemblance to actual persons, living or dead, events, or locales is entirely coincidental.

For information regarding permissions, contact Growing Field Books at:

Growing Field Books
2012 Pacific Ct.
Ft. Collins, CO 80528

Written by Mark E. Hoog. Illustrated and designed by Mark W. Adams. Edited by Jennifer Thomas.

Publisher's Cataloging-in-Publication
(Provided by Quality Books, Inc.)

Hoog, Mark E.
Treasure Island : a Growing Field adventure / by Mark E. Hoog ; illustrated by Mark Adams.
p. cm.

SUMMARY: In search of Treasure Island, Pete learns to adjust and "set his sail" to overcome adversity as he pursues his magical journey called life.

LCCN: 2010934792
ISBN-13: 978-0-9770391-4-2

1. Leadership--Juvenile fiction. 2. Character--Juvenile fiction.
3. Self-esteem--Juvenile fiction. 4. Sailing--Juvenile fiction.
[1. Leadership--Fiction. 2. Character--Fiction.
3. Self-esteem--Fiction. 4. Sailing--Fiction.] I. Adams, Mark, 1970- ill. II. Title.

PZ7.H76335Tre 2011
[Fic]
QBI10-600182

Recommended for ages 4 and up.

Printed in China / March 2011

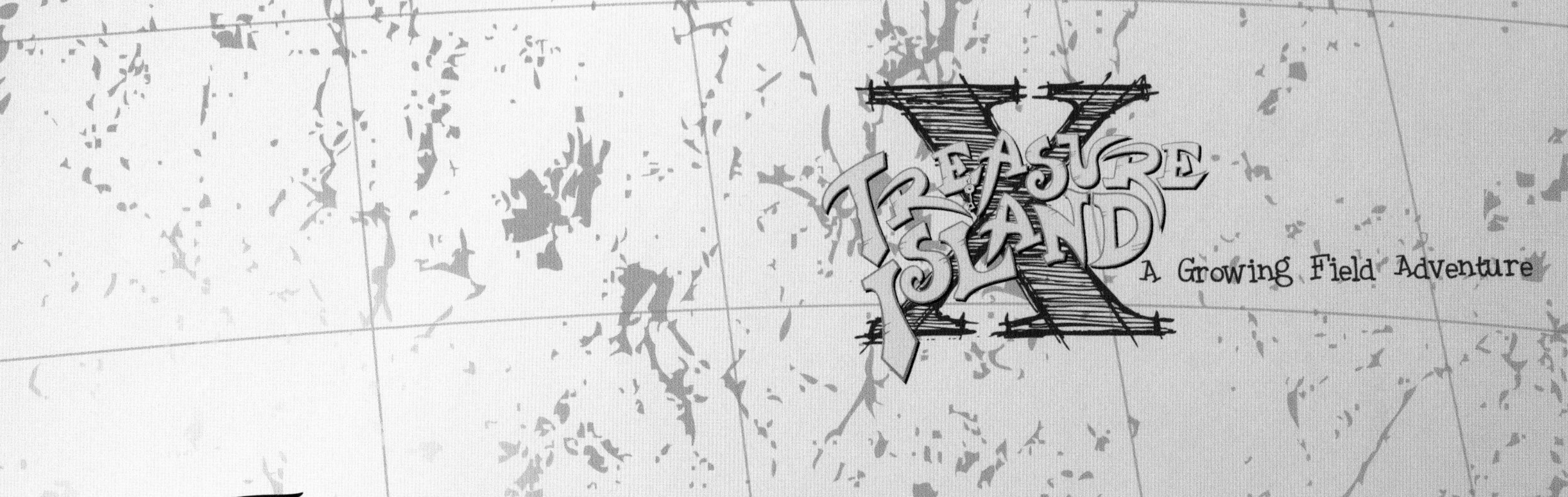

"The sea is dangerous and its storms terrible,
but these obstacles have never been sufficient reason
to remain ashore...unlike the mediocre,
intrepid spirits seek victory over those things that seem impossible...
it is with an iron will that they embark on the most daring
of all endeavors...to meet the shadowy future without fear
and conquer the unkown."

– Ferdinand Magellan

Spectacular children live in the magical town of Walden.

Some are tall, some short. Some have light hair and others dark.
Some are big, others small. Some wear glasses and others do not.
The children in Walden are just like you!

So, you may ask, what makes these children so spectacular? The answer is found in the questions they ask and the answers they discover in a magical place called the *Growing Field*.

It is here where the wise sage *Nightingale* mysteriously appears to share ideas about making their dreams in life come true.

Nightingale appears in many forms, to creatively show Walden children how to live life without limit. Some say *Nightingale's* ideas can be used forever!

The best part: the children from Walden love to share their *Growing Field* discoveries with you.

Standing at the Walden Marina, watching the boats drift lazily on the water,
Pete had no idea that today was the day *his* life would change forever.

Reading the back of one boat, Pete couldn't help but wonder:
What if there really were a Treasure Island?
Would I have the courage and tenacity to find it?
Or would obstacles stand in my way?

Pete saw a small dinghy approaching in the distance.
As it neared, he saw his older brother, Maxx, sitting inside.

Pete reached out for his big brother's hand and climbed into the boat.

"You need to expect challenges in life," Maxx told him.
"Also expect to overcome them. It is life's challenges that make you who you are and reveal your true character. I learned that in my own *Growing Field* adventure when I was your age!"

"On your adventure," Maxx said, "you must seek out *Nightingale* and find the magical Treasure Island."

Pete nodded excitedly. He was ready!

Maxx stepped out of the boat and gave it a small push away from the dock. "Now," he said, "prepare yourself for the adventure of a lifetime!"

Pete picked up the oars, more than ready to try.
A distant buoy soon caught his eye.
He rowed toward it quickly, to see what it said.
That's when he saw it…written in red.

Pete needed a vessel, to Treasure Island to sail—
a craft of epic proportions, one fit for this tale.
Now launched on his journey, everything changed right away.
That's why Pete's pirate adventure is still told to this day.

The dinghy transformed;
it grew teak wooden rails,
along with masts, ropes, and pulleys
to steer all of the sails.

A boat tall and strong, a hull true and tough—
built to handle the sea, should it begin to get rough.

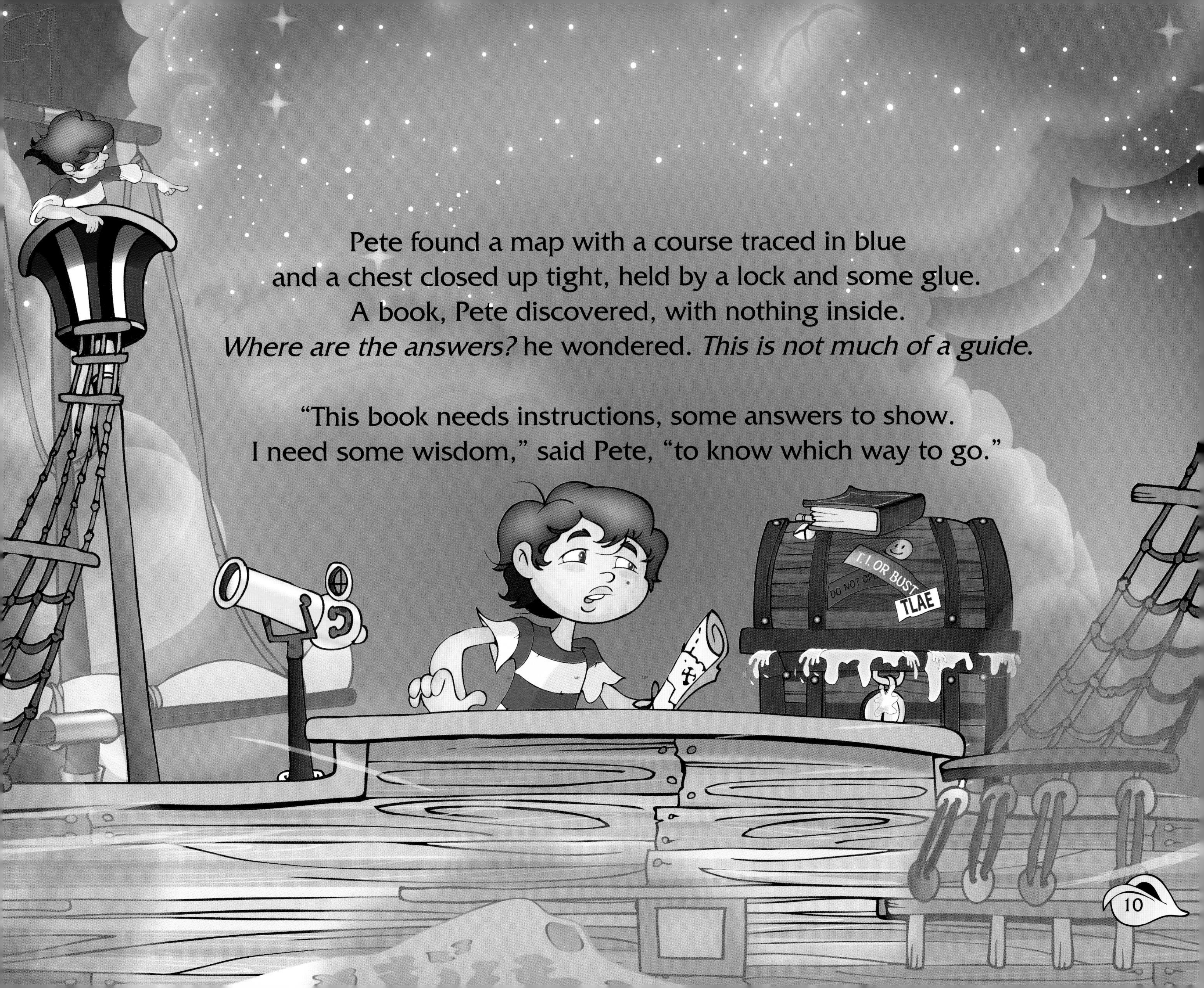

Pete found a map with a course traced in blue
and a chest closed up tight, held by a lock and some glue.
A book, Pete discovered, with nothing inside.
Where are the answers? he wondered. *This is not much of a guide.*

"This book needs instructions, some answers to show.
I need some wisdom," said Pete, "to know which way to go."

Treasure Island's my goal! Pete decided to write.
The tale of Treasure Island began—there, on that night.

Lucky, penned Pete, *of my current direction.*
It's perfect, in fact—there's no need for correction.
This boat, my position, the course that I'm on—
Treasure Island awaits. What could go wrong?

Trouble loomed; obstacles waited ahead.
But Pete closed his eyes, and rested his head.
With much to be done, Pete should have worked faster.
Instead he did nothing and sailed straight toward disaster.

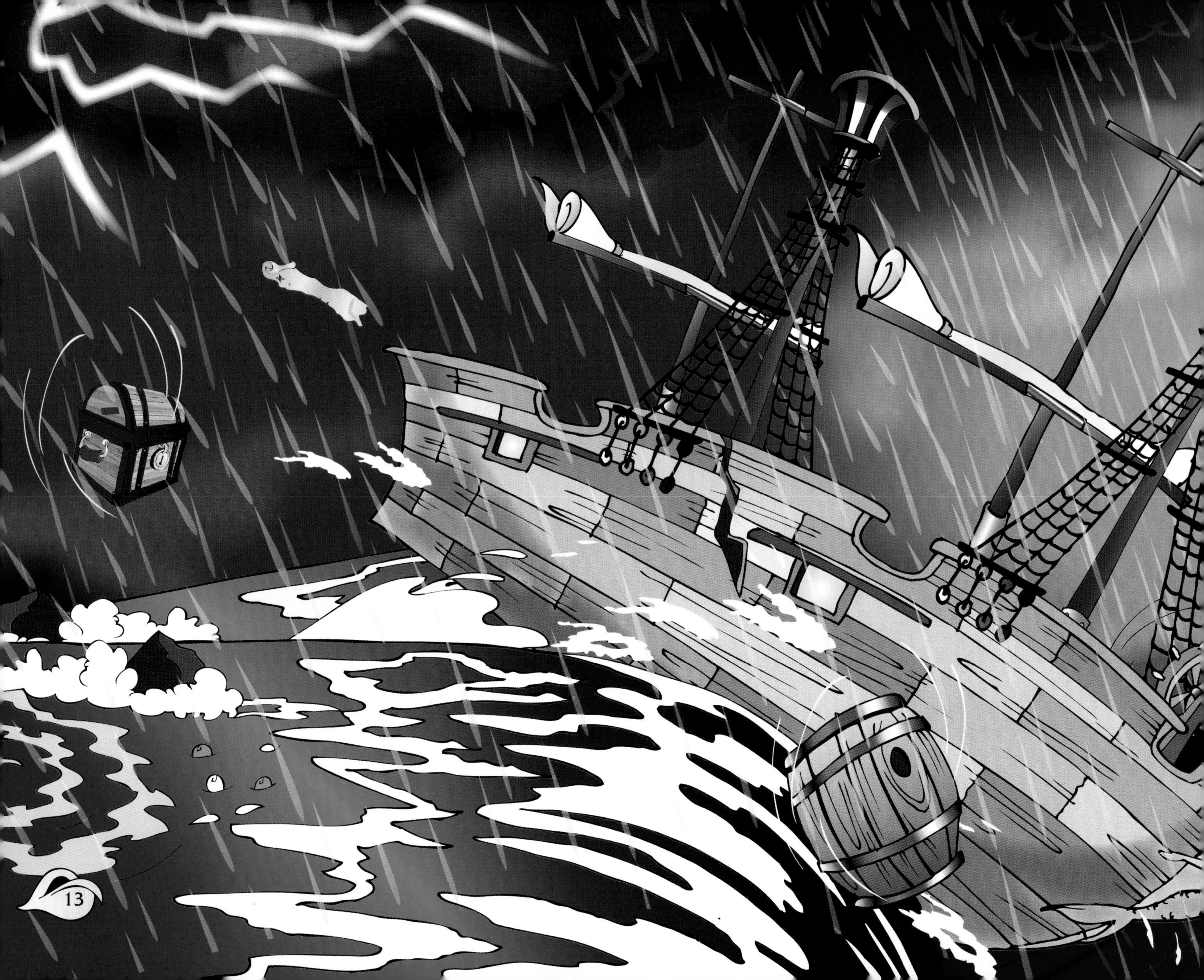

When he awoke later, Pete knew things weren't right,
but he had no idea all that would happen this night.
The sky filled with mist, making Pete blind.
"Treasure Island," he said, "will now be hard to find."

Pete's boat drifted faster; he could not make it stop.
Over a waterfall it teetered, and then started to drop.
The sea grew angry. Rain flew in Pete's face.
Huge rocks seemed to spring up all over the place.

The boat rocked to the left, and it rolled to the right—
surrounded by waves, all looking to fight.
Thunder, then lightning, it was fear Pete now felt.
He yelled into the night: "Somebody please help!"

All went quiet. Pete's voyage had gone terribly wrong.
The storm was too violent, and had lasted too long.

I am not sure, Pete wrote, *to this place how I came.*
It can't be my fault; there must be someone to blame.
The wind was the problem, for it blew me off course.
It isn't my fault—the air was the source.
Or the rain that fell down, so heavily flowing—
it would not let me see just where I was going.

"Fault lies with others!" Pete claimed, dumping sand from his shoe.
"I could have done nothing more. I am *sure* this is true."

Pete didn't know it, but his next step was key.
It's the one all must take, if dreams are to be.

Pete brushed himself off, and he pulled up his socks.
He gave a tug on his bootstraps and started to walk.

That's when the voice came…from where Pete couldn't tell.
But looking down toward his feet, he saw an odd-looking shell.

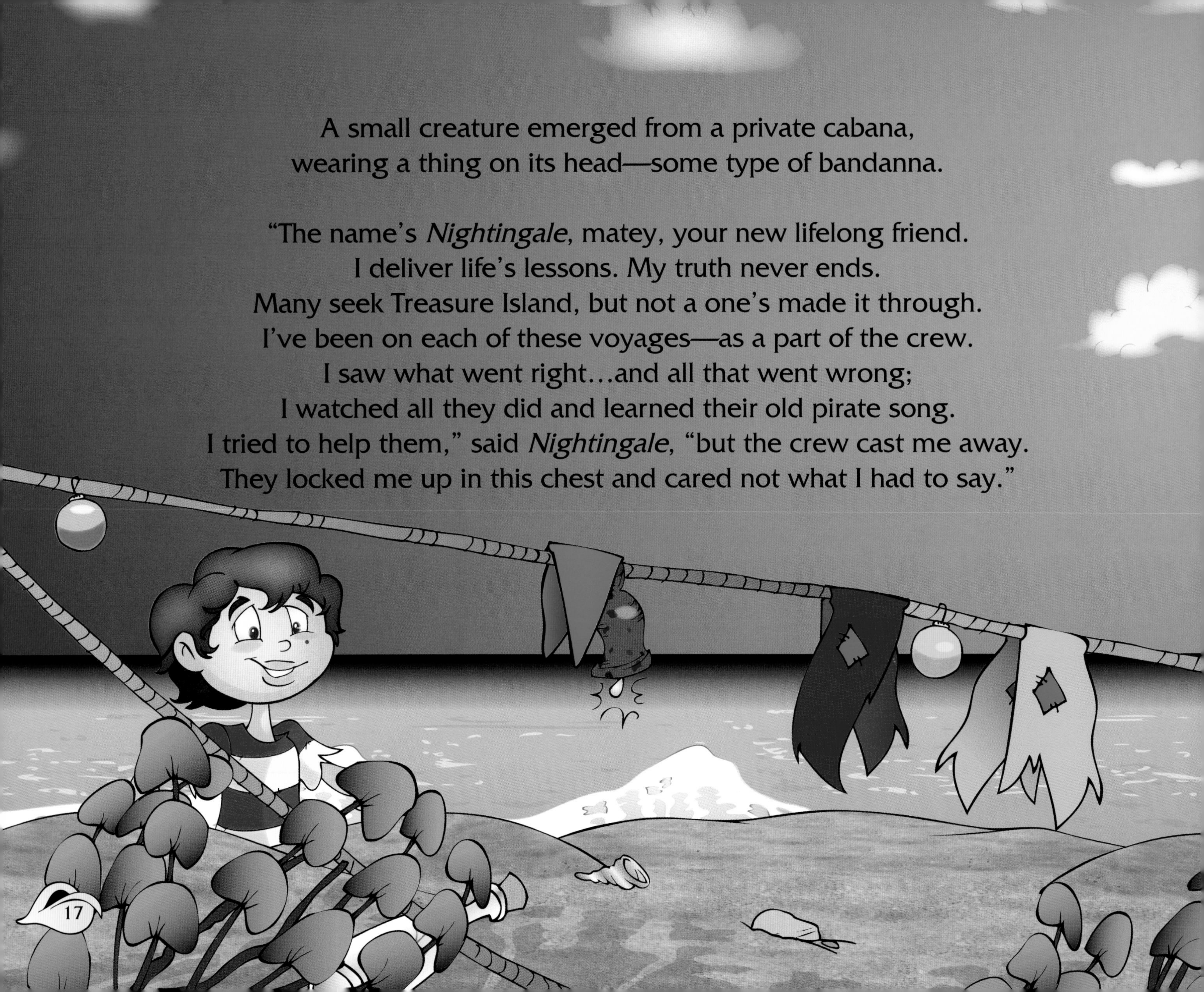

A small creature emerged from a private cabana,
wearing a thing on its head—some type of bandanna.

"The name's *Nightingale*, matey, your new lifelong friend.
I deliver life's lessons. My truth never ends.
Many seek Treasure Island, but not a one's made it through.
I've been on each of these voyages—as a part of the crew.
I saw what went right…and all that went wrong;
I watched all they did and learned their old pirate song.
I tried to help them," said *Nightingale*, "but the crew cast me away.
They locked me up in this chest and cared not what I had to say."

"For years I've been waiting, to speak and be heard;
to meet a new pirate who wouldn't think me absurd.
There are secrets I'll tell you, if you'd like to know.
They'll lead you to treasure. Would you like to go?"

"Pete's the name," said our hero, finding a smile.
"Well, Pete," said *Nightingale*, "let's walk for a while.
Can you overcome *your* challenges? For this answer you yearn.
Here comes the secret..." whispered *Nightingale*. "Now, listen and learn!"

"All seek treasure," said *Nightingale*. "It's life greatest gift.
Each one's treasure is different, for which we search and we sift.
Some want great achievements; they look for success.
But sometimes in the process, they create quite a mess.
I'll show you examples, from which you can learn.
Take notes if you want; it's wisdom you'll earn."

Pete picked up his journal, another entry to make:
Perhaps there's a lesson in making mistakes.

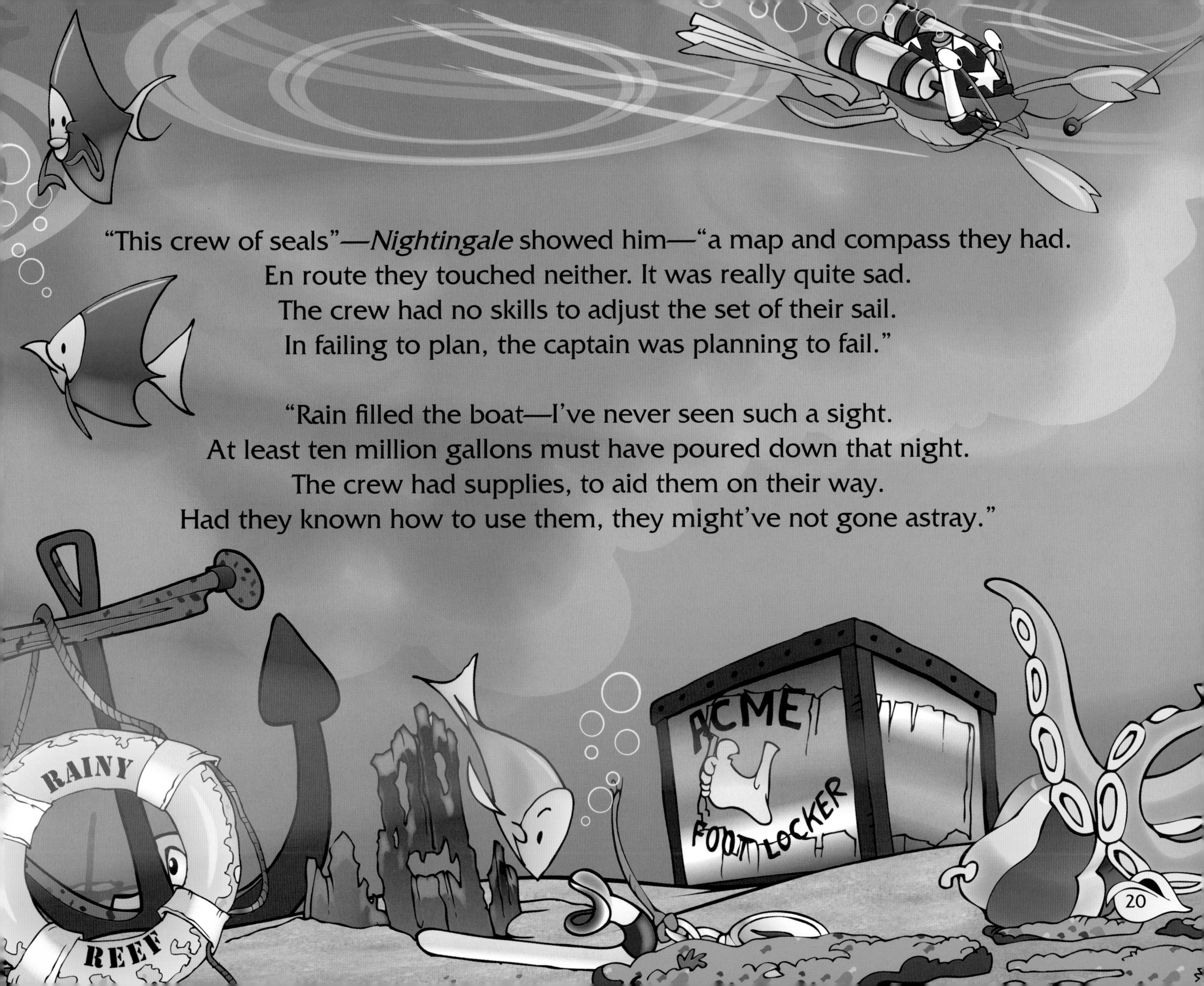

"This crew of seals"—*Nightingale* showed him—"a map and compass they had.
En route they touched neither. It was really quite sad.
The crew had no skills to adjust the set of their sail.
In failing to plan, the captain was planning to fail."

"Rain filled the boat—I've never seen such a sight.
At least ten million gallons must have poured down that night.
The crew had supplies, to aid them on their way.
Had they known how to use them, they might've not gone astray."

"Nothing worthwhile comes easy, so when your treasure's in sight,
remember your dream," said *Nightingale*, "and why for it you'll fight."

"See *this* boat?" *Nightingale* pointed. "Here in pieces today.
With Treasure Island in sight, rocks blocked the ship's way.
A crew full of turtles, their course could have changed—
but the captain did nothing. Now, isn't that strange?"

"A telescope they had, to learn what was ahead.
The crew stayed on deck, though—just playing instead.
The boulders we hit: some we *could* have sailed around.
The ship broke to pieces; no treasure was found."

Not taking charge seemed to be their mistake.
You must pay attention: a conscious choice you must make.
Don't drift. Find a purpose—steer when you can.
Most importantly, wrote Pete, *you must have a plan.*

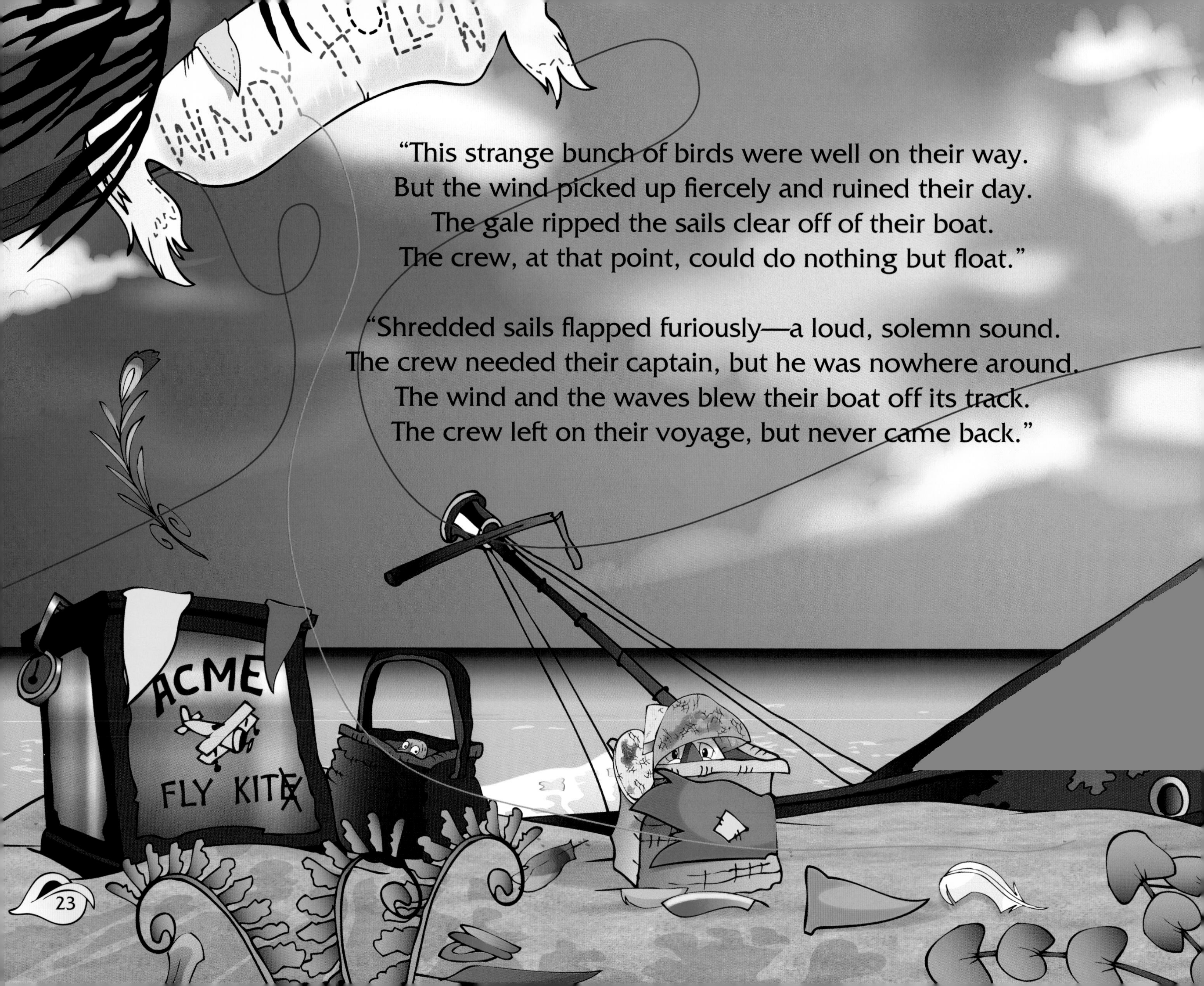

"This strange bunch of birds were well on their way.
But the wind picked up fiercely and ruined their day.
The gale ripped the sails clear off of their boat.
The crew, at that point, could do nothing but float."

"Shredded sails flapped furiously—a loud, solemn sound.
The crew needed their captain, but he was nowhere around.
The wind and the waves blew their boat off its track.
The crew left on their voyage, but never came back."

The wind will blow strong, wrote Pete, *and on each name will call.*
Recognize that in life, the wind blows on us all.
But no matter the problem, no matter the source,
I'll try, Pete now vowed, *to stay always on course.*

Stay on track! Pete added, writing this one down twice.
I am the captain. This is a great piece of advice.

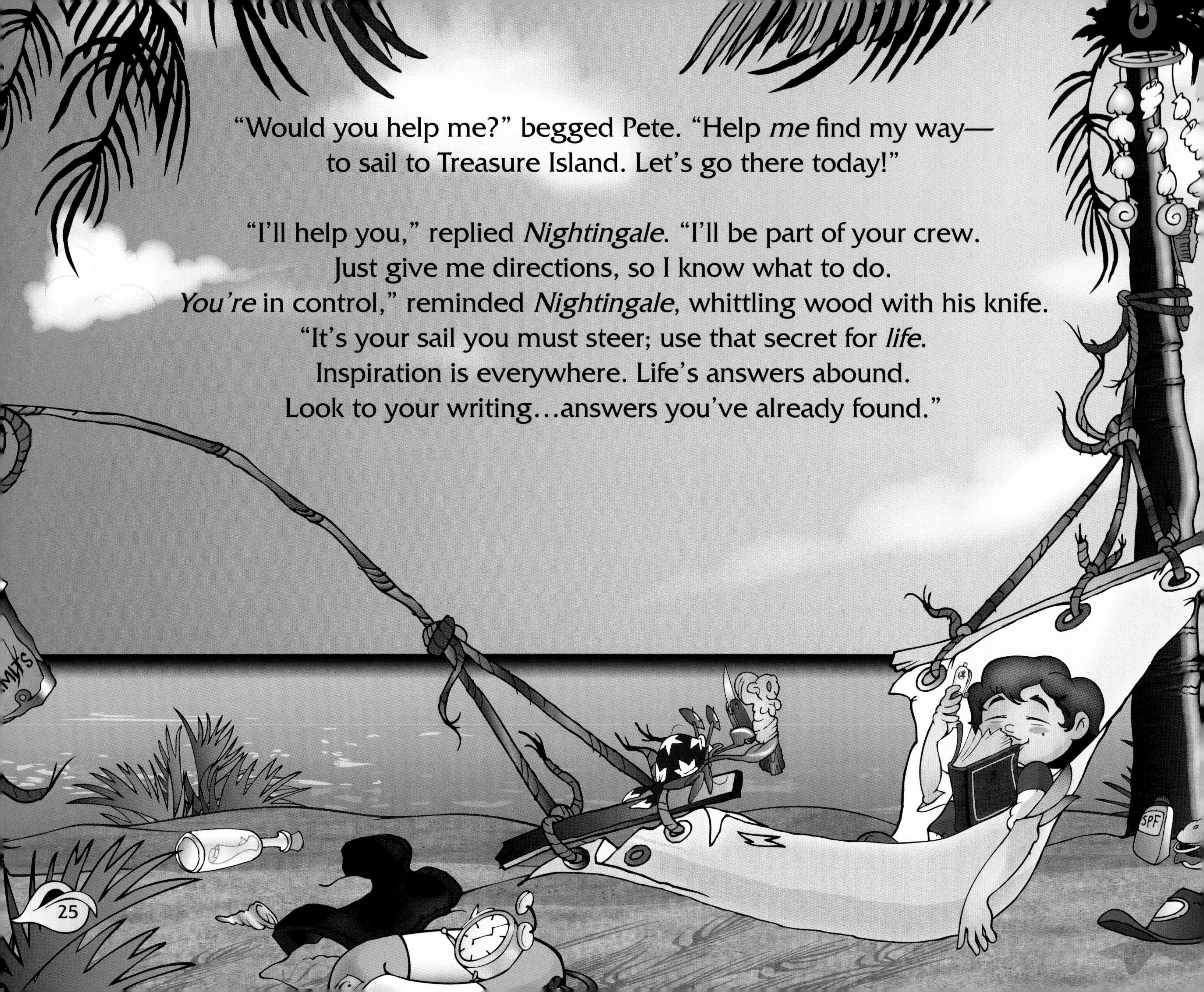

"Would you help me?" begged Pete. "Help *me* find my way—
to sail to Treasure Island. Let's go there today!"

"I'll help you," replied *Nightingale*. "I'll be part of your crew.
Just give me directions, so I know what to do.
You're in control," reminded *Nightingale*, whittling wood with his knife.
"It's your sail you must steer; use that secret for *life*.
Inspiration is everywhere. Life's answers abound.
Look to your writing…answers you've already found."

Pete's journal—he realized—held all he'd hoped to discover.
Pete called it "The Code" and wrote that right on the cover.
He reviewed it again; all the words were so true.
Then he rose to take action—he knew *just* what to do.

First, with his map, he found a place in the shade.
And then, with his pen, important changes were made.

"I know of my challenges. I'll map each attack.
I'll need an old salty crew to help keep me on track.
My time has come," Pete said, now free of fear.
Nightingale smiled as Pete whispered a plan in his ear...

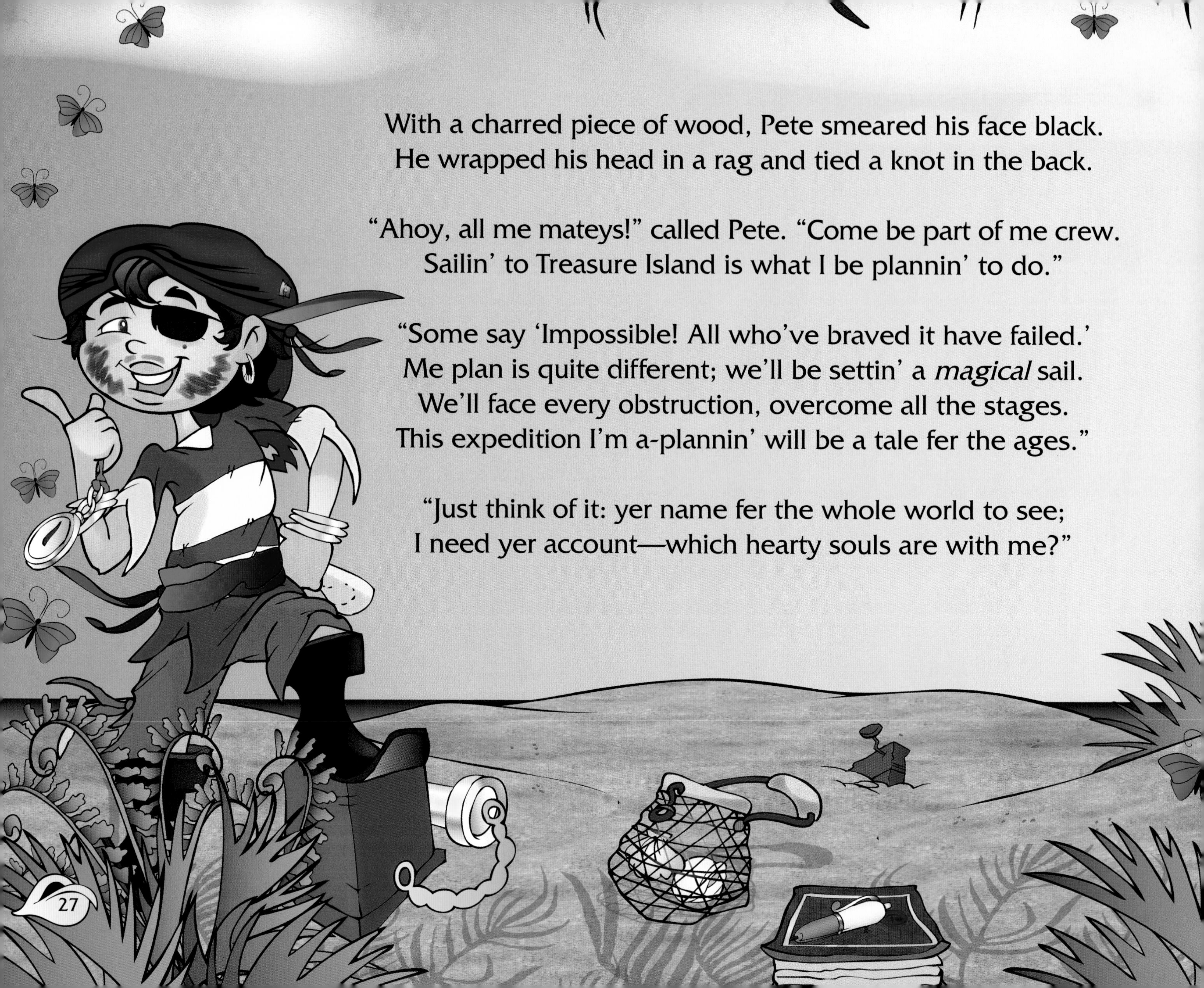

With a charred piece of wood, Pete smeared his face black.
He wrapped his head in a rag and tied a knot in the back.

“Ahoy, all me mateys!” called Pete. “Come be part of me crew.
Sailin’ to Treasure Island is what I be plannin’ to do.”

“Some say ‘Impossible! All who’ve braved it have failed.’
Me plan is quite different; we’ll be settin’ a *magical* sail.
We’ll face every obstruction, overcome all the stages.
This expedition I’m a-plannin’ will be a tale fer the ages.”

“Just think of it: yer name fer the whole world to see;
I need yer account—which hearty souls are with me?”

From out of the brush and under rocks they all came.
Buccaneers smiled to their captain as each told him their name.

"Ahoy, me crew," welcomed Pete. "Here's what must be done.
It's time fer leavin' this islan'. It is *our* time that's come!
Each crew member's key, if Treasure Islan' we're to find.
Lookin' at each of ya, the word 'perfect' comes to me mind."

"Me mateys," said Pete, "ye must get to work fast.
Use these parts from the boats that have failed in the past."

Alongside his crew, the captain taught and instructed.
Using just the right pieces, a new boat was constructed.
"Use these tools," offered Pete. "'Ere's some nails and me glue.
Our ship won't be pretty, but it's the best we can do."

"Yo ho ho!" Nightingale hummed his old pirate song.
The crew labored hard; their craft was coming along.

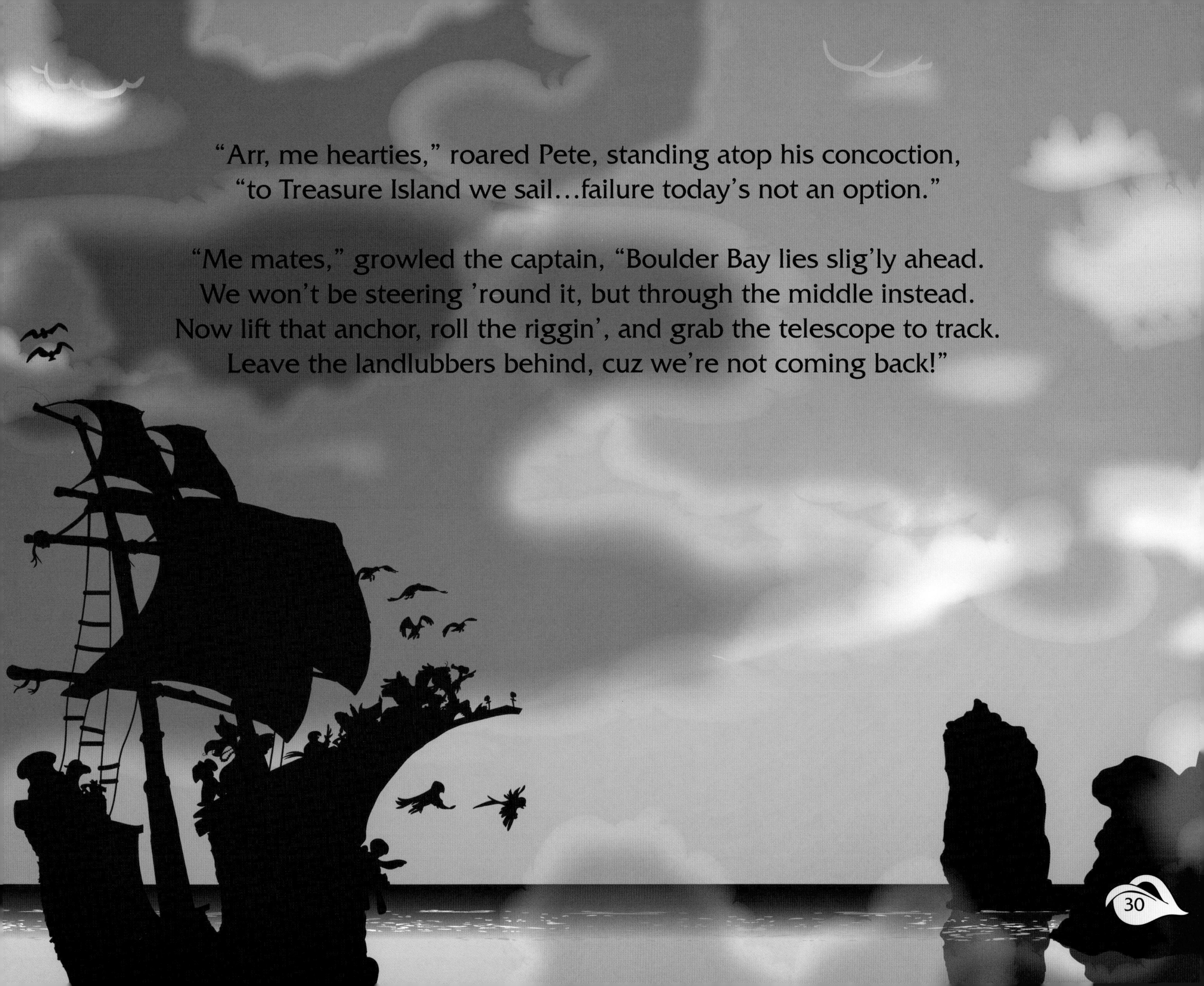

"Arr, me hearties," roared Pete, standing atop his concoction,
"to Treasure Island we sail…failure today's not an option."

"Me mates," growled the captain, "Boulder Bay lies slig'ly ahead.
We won't be steering 'round it, but through the middle instead.
Now lift that anchor, roll the riggin', and grab the telescope to track.
Leave the landlubbers behind, cuz we're not coming back!"

When the first rock was hit, the telescope rolled o'er the side.
Some turtles dove to stop it, but it sank in the tide.

The turtles cried out, "Now there's not a thing we can do!"
"Never argue for yer limitations," boomed Pete, "or they'll become true!
Now, me scallywag, instead, find the reasons ye can.
I'm needin' yer best; this is all part of me plan."

Charging through Boulder Bay, more large rocks drew near.
That's when Pete heard the first turtle fly right past his ear.

From high on the masts, the crew began their attack.
Each dove at the rocks, and then doubled back.
"Argh, me mateys," yelled Pete, "continue ye must.
Me airborne brigade, turn these rocks into dust!"

"Yo ho ho!" the turtles sang as they fought.
"These rocks," all agreed, "were not as tough as we thought."

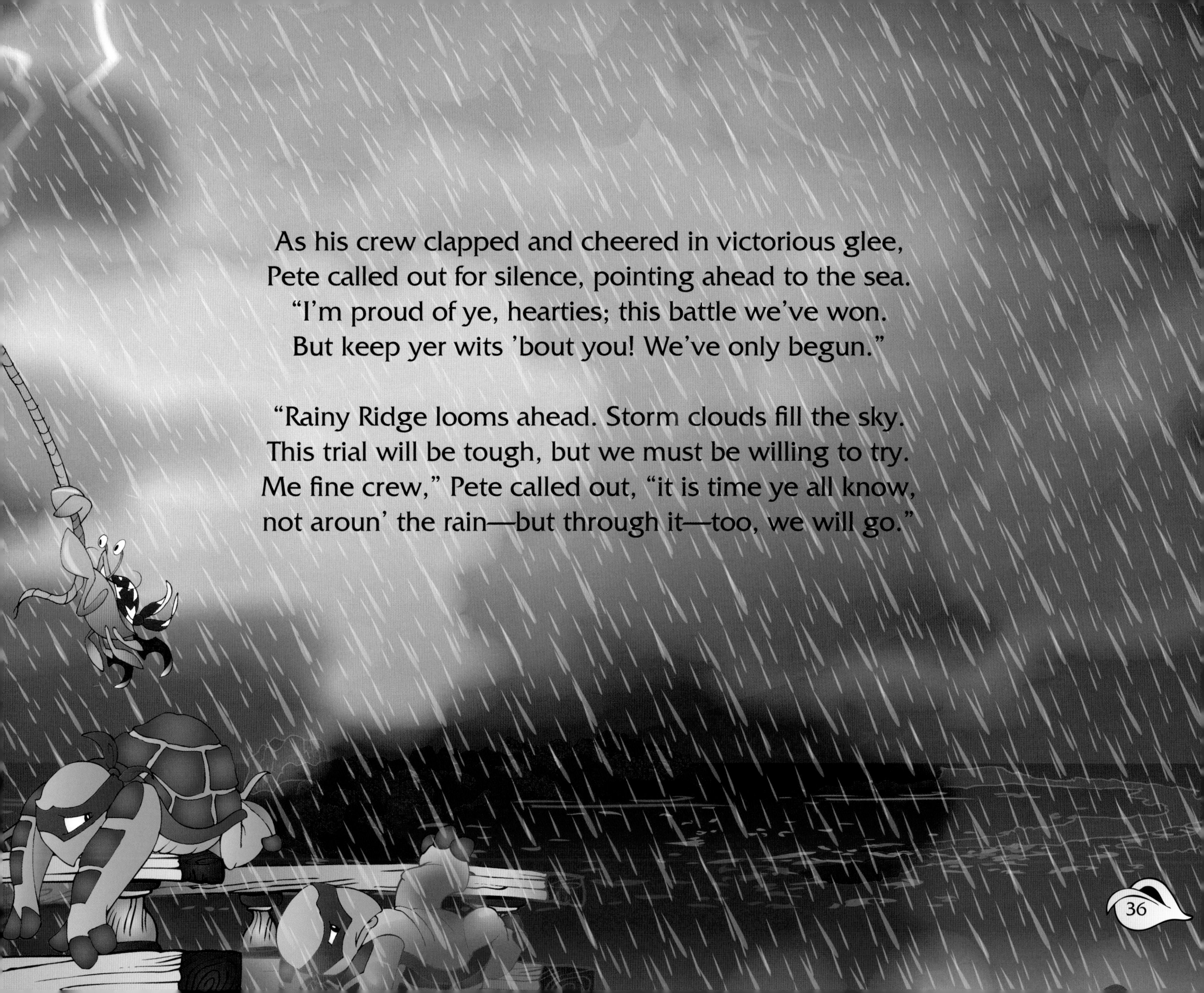

As his crew clapped and cheered in victorious glee,
Pete called out for silence, pointing ahead to the sea.
"I'm proud of ye, hearties; this battle we've won.
But keep yer wits 'bout you! We've only begun."

"Rainy Ridge looms ahead. Storm clouds fill the sky.
This trial will be tough, but we must be willing to try.
Me fine crew," Pete called out, "it is time ye all know,
not aroun' the rain—but through it—too, we will go."

The rain poured down ahead; the trap, it was set.
It appeared the whole world was about to get wet.

"Seals, look to your compass," cried Pete. "Yer course ye must check."
But as a young seal tried to grab it, the compass rolled off the deck.

"With no compass," said the seals, "our course we'll ne'er find."
"Use yer *inner* compass," said Pete. "Set the course in yer mind.
In yer own True North, believe," Pete said, "and never stop thinkin'.
Now, do what ye can to stop us from sinkin'!"

Gathering their gear, the seals became all they could be.
With supplies from the past, they worked on the high sea.
"Yo ho ho!" sang the seals, as they scattered about.
With tubes, buckets, and hoses, they pushed the rain water out.

"This rain's not a reason," said the seals, "to lose sight of our way.
In where we are going, we *do* have a say!"

"Windy Hollow," Pete said, "is the next challenge to be met.
Ye must all understand: 'twill be our toughest course yet."
The wind howled fiercely, tearing the sails to shreds.
"Shiver me timbers," said Pete. "Find a new way instead."

"Ahoy there! Ye *all* must do all ye can do.
Without you and yer talents, we'll ne'er get through.
Repair the canvas, so with wind, our sails we can fill.
It is now time to say: 'Aye, I can and I will!'"

"We must *steer*; that's what this challenge is for.
This ship is *ours*—we must get it to shore."

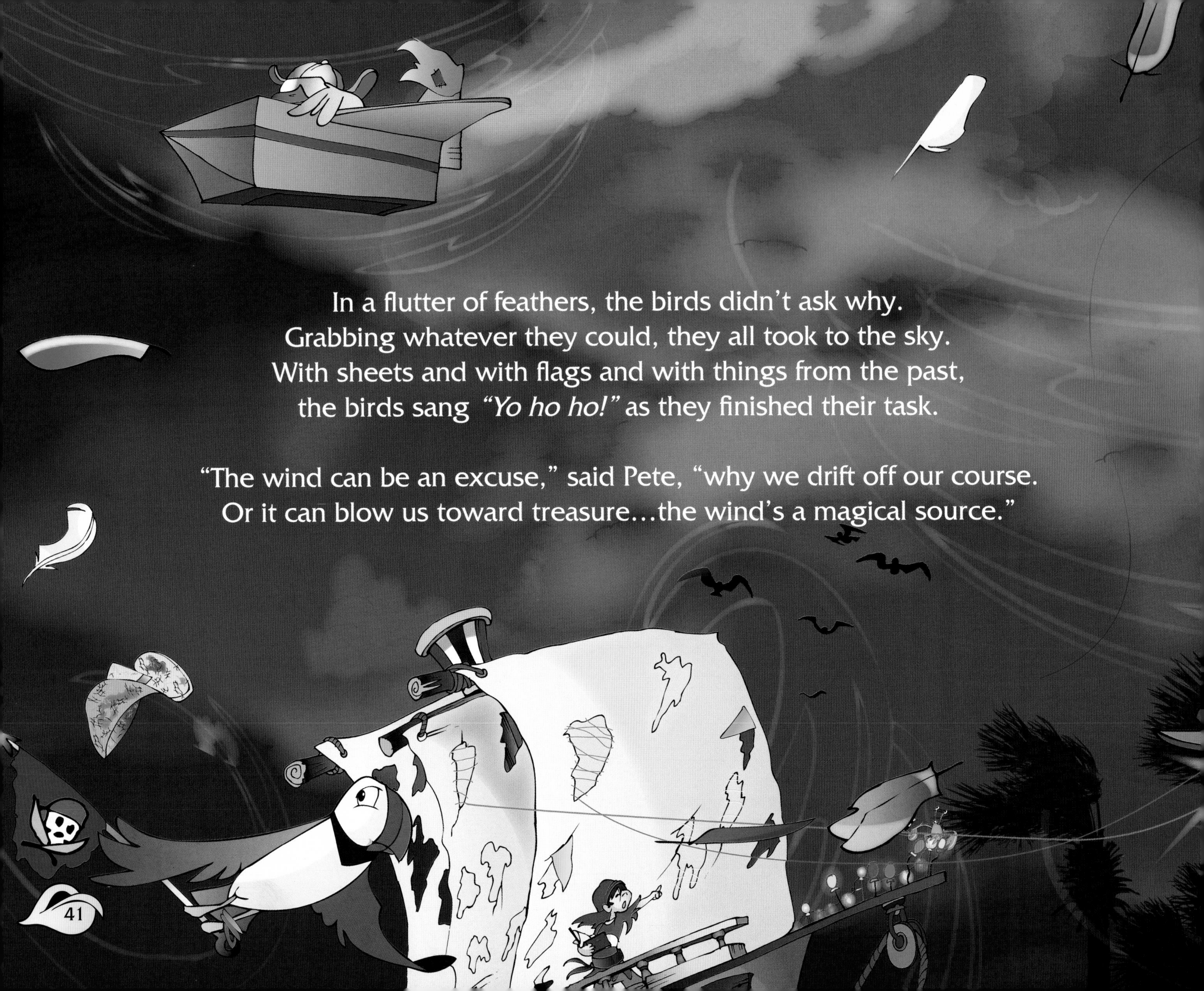

In a flutter of feathers, the birds didn't ask why.
Grabbing whatever they could, they all took to the sky.
With sheets and with flags and with things from the past,
the birds sang *"Yo ho ho!"* as they finished their task.

"The wind can be an excuse," said Pete, "why we drift off our course.
Or it can blow us toward treasure…the wind's a magical source."

What waited next for our crew was the worst kind of weather.
You see the rocks, rain, and wind agreed to all work together.
Against all three at once, it seemed they'd never make land.
As the boat pulled apart, Pete found one last order to command.

“Smartly, me friends, the Pirate Code we now know:
In life we can steer *anywhere* we choose to go.
The time’s now upon us—make yer dreams come true.
I give one last instruction and ask this task now of you:
All hands ahoy. Ye birds, find a way now—
grab ropes from me riggin’ and fly up from the bow.
And you there, me seals, ye must trust now me plan;
with this tank fill these tubes, as much as ye can.
And me turtles, one more trick, now ye must learn:
tie this string to yer shells and attach tight to the stern.”

The clouds became darker; the wind doubled in speed.
The rocks became larger—our friends were in trouble, indeed.
The sand grew beneath them; their boat was now stuck.
The rain came down heavier…and then lightning struck!

Time ran out. The rocks and waves started to fall.
It was then Pete's crew worked his plan…

...and flew HIGH over it all!

Soaring over their obstacles, Pete could barely believe.
He pulled out The Code and added the final lesson received:

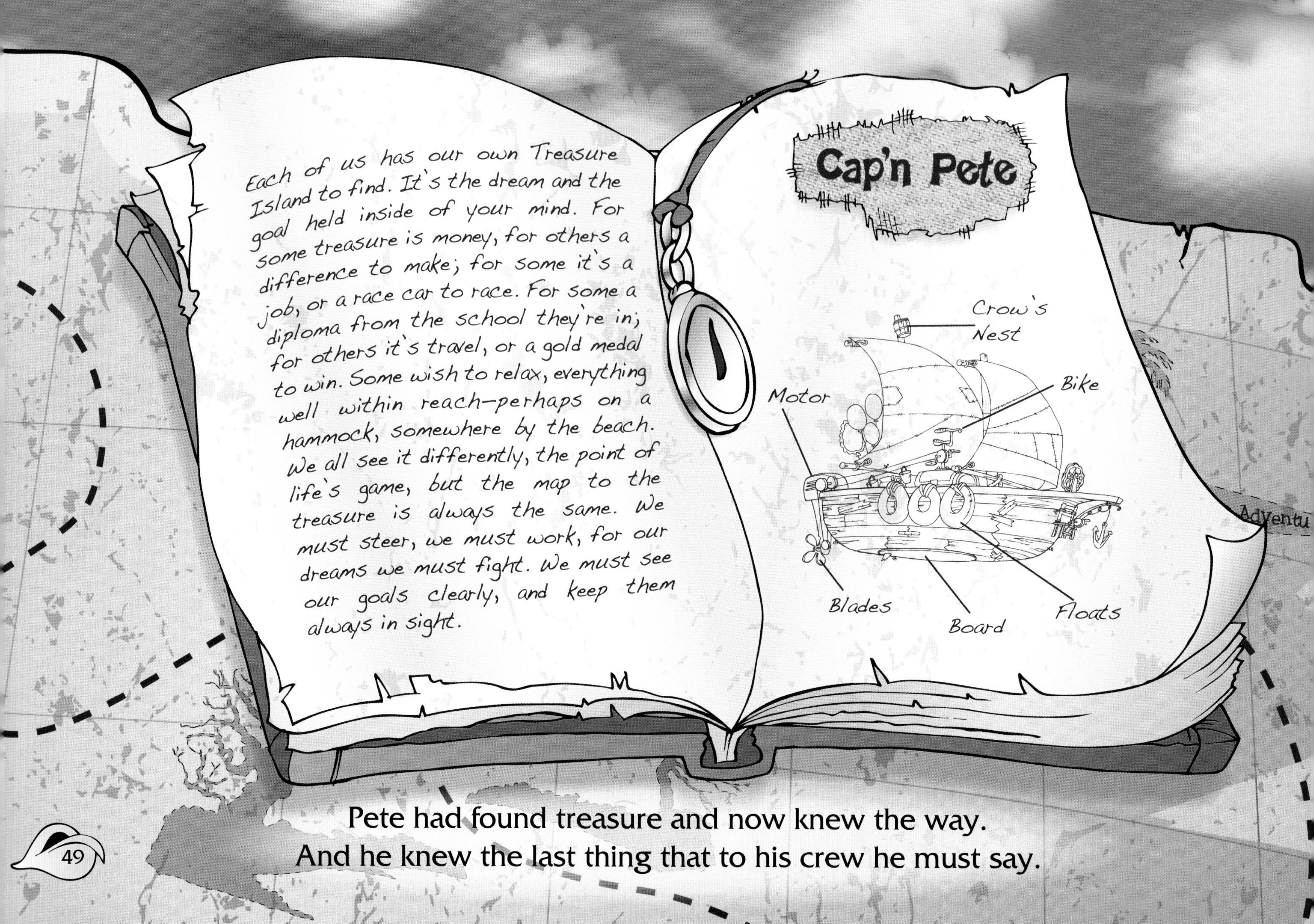

Pete had found treasure and now knew the way.
And he knew the last thing that to his crew he must say.

Pete called to his shipmates: "To honor how ye've all grown..."
He threw strips from the sails. "Here's a headband of yer own!
Let it remind you, the wind will continue to blow,
but we adjust our own sail—the Pirate Code we now know."

"*Yo ho ho*, me mates! There is no mistake.
Ye've each set yer own magical sail, and now yer Treasure Island..."

. . . awaits!"
MACHINE
WINNER!

Pete opened his eyes and found himself back on the dock.
Feeling something in his shoe, Pete knelt down and removed a small shell.
He held it to his ear and hear a soft voice from within:

*"Don't get discouraged by your challenges in life.
Instead, look at them as opportunities to adjust the set of your own sail.
I look forward to watching you command your way through the river of life.
Arrrr...I love you, little pirate."*

Pete knew he would never again worry about what circumstances arose, because he was the captain of his own destiny.

"Thank you, *Nightingale,*" he whispered. "I will keep you with me forever. I love you, too."

Discussion Seeds for *Treasure Island*

Each of us pursues a different treasure in life. *Treasure Island* illustrates for children that, regardless of what goals they pursue, they need not fear the winds that blow along the way. They need only learn to set a strong sail.

Leaders understand that every worthwhile goal will bring adversity to be overcome. We must teach our children to "pull themselves up by their bootstraps" and to take responsibility for navigating their challenges.

Help your child create a treasure map for success by asking him or her to:

 Develop five goals for the future

 Think of obstacles that may arise

 Explore ways to overcome these obstacles

 Begin capturing life inspiration and ideas in his or her own *Growing Field Journal*

Teach your son or daughter to set a magical sail, to prepare for the greatest adventure of all…life!

Today is a spectacular day to teach your child to say, "Aye…I can and I will."

Embark on a treasure hunt for success with your child today!

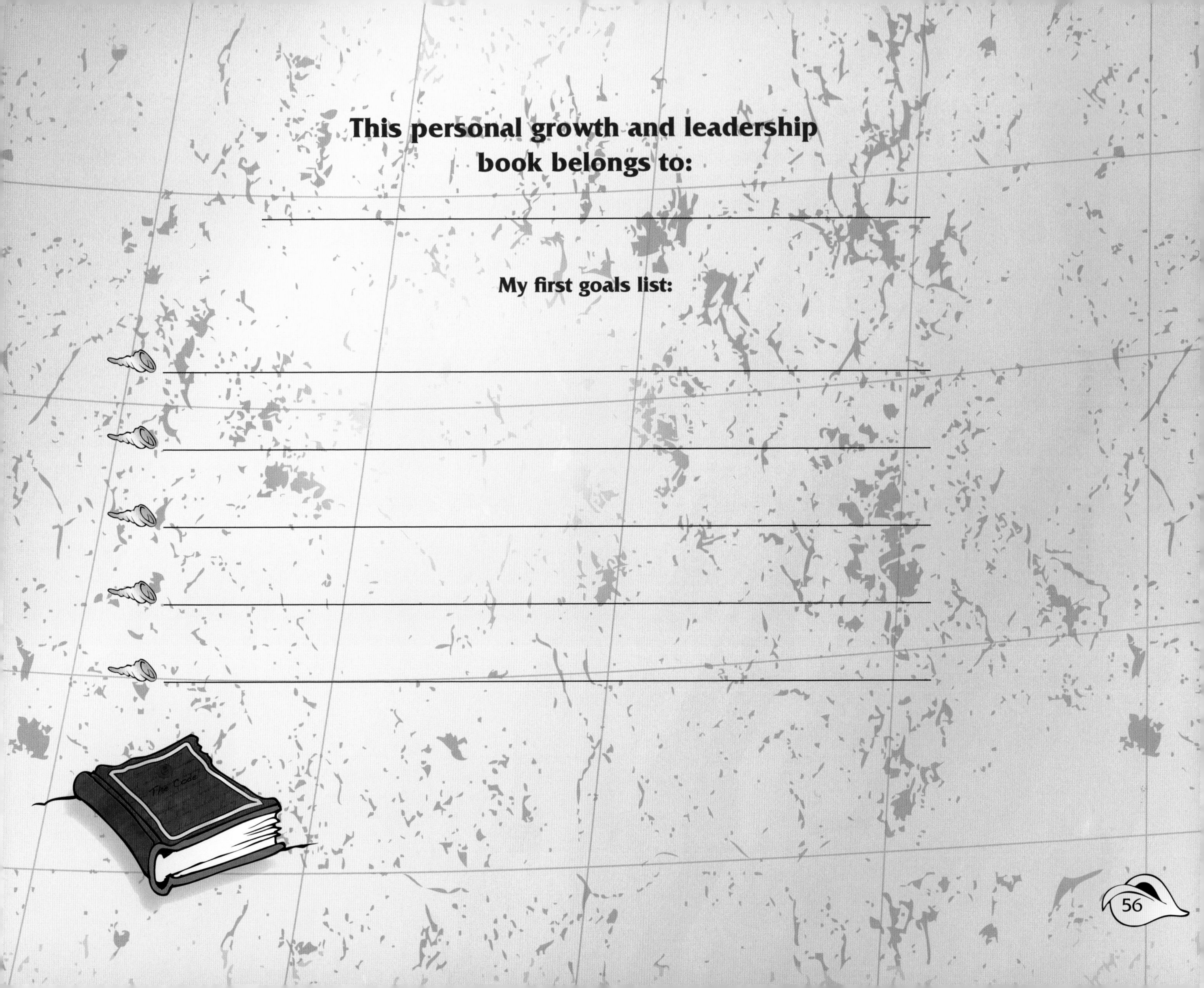

This personal growth and leadership book belongs to:

____

My first goals list:

____

____

____

____

____

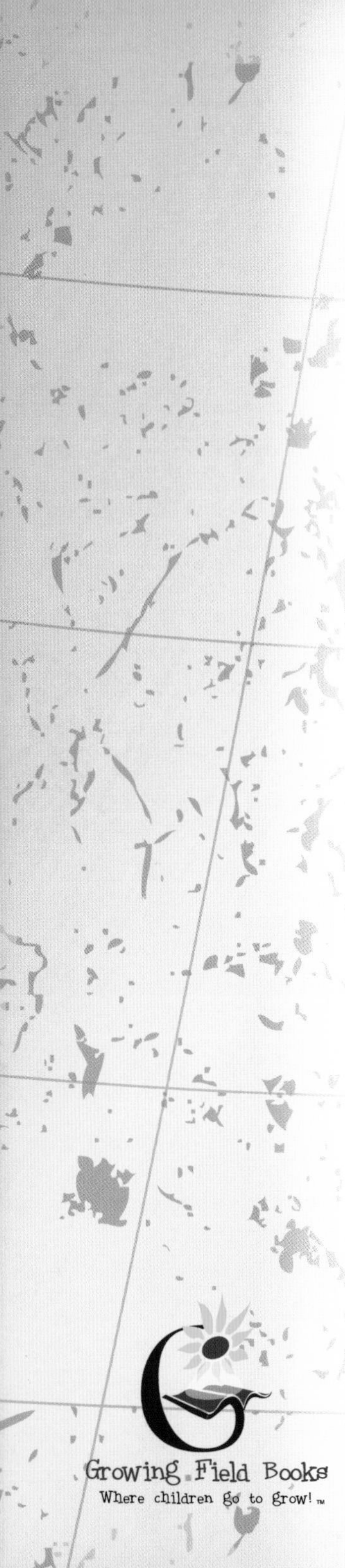

Welcome to the Growing Field!

Read what leaders are saying about their magical journey through the Growing Field...

"Mark Hoog's book delivers an important message to young readers: If a dream is worth having, it's worth working for. If you believe in yourself and are dedicated to achieving your goals, you can accomplish anything—all it takes is hard work and determination. I encourage you to follow the example of the children in *Dream Machine* and make your dreams come true."

—William Jefferson Clinton, 42nd President of the United States of America

"A walk through Mark Hoog's Growing Field series is a wonderful and creative way for any adult to help grow a child's self-esteem, character, and love of reading. Everyone can benefit from the seeds to be found in the Growing Field."

—Richard Riley, U.S. Secretary of Education

"Mark Hoog is doing the most important work in America today—growing our children. With Magic and Treasure and Dreams and Songs and Gifts, he's helping them learn to lead. Mark's work is one of the best gifts you can give both children and adults. The Growing Field series MUST be the next thing you read and share with others."

—W. Mitchell, Top Motivational Speaker U.S./Australia

The Seeds of the Growing Field...

Following the events of 9–11, including the death of his close friend and colleague Jason Dahl—Captain of Flight 93, which crashed in Pennsylvania—author Mark Hoog struggled to find meaning and purpose in a challenging time.

In Hoog's darkest moment, powerful thoughts from his past literary readings—everything from Aristotle to Thoreau to Confucius to Tony Robbins—presented themselves to him in the form of simple bedtime stories for children. Each story delivered ideas associated with some of our greatest leaders and philosophers, at a level simple enough to introduce children to the concepts of personal growth and leadership. The Growing Field series was born.

Today, the Growing Field series is enjoyed around the world and is recognized for its motivational and inspirational message to youth. The Growing Field serves to let children know we believe in their life—and reminds adults that it is never too early to teach our children the ideas and behaviors associated with living life without limit!

Seeds of Success are found in the Growing Field!

Children of all ages will delight in learning valuable life skills from the nationally acclaimed Growing Field personal growth and leadership book series.

The Growing Field introduces children to ideas and beliefs that will enable them to ***Live Life without Limit!***

Your Song introduces children to their unique gifts and talents.

Dream Machine invites children to dream about their possibilities.

Field of Dreams teaches children to cultivate the "Seeds of Success" planted by their dreams.

Growing Field Journal guides children through the journaling process, empowering them to captain their own ship as they navigate life.

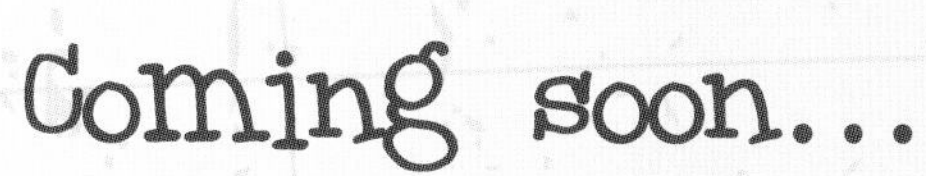

Coming soon...

Magic Mountain  The Gift

ORDER at WWW.GROWINGFIELD.COM OR anywhere fine books are sold!
TOLL free 1-866-465-4211

We may encounter many defeats…
but we must not be defeated.
—Maya Angelou

Those who want to succeed will find a way;
those who don't will find an excuse!
—Leo Aguila

Rocky Ridge

The person who goes farthest is generally
the one who is willing to do and dare.
The sure-thing boat never gets far from shore.
—Dale Carnegie

The pessimist complains about the wind;
the optimist expects it to change;
the realist adjusts the sails.
—William A. Ward

I'm not afraid of storms,
for I'm learning how to sail my ship.
—Louisa May Alcott

Rainy Reef

I have never encountered a person who
achieved anything that didn't require
overcoming obstacles.
Expect them.
—Lou Holtz

The bravest are surely those who have
the clearest vision of what is before them,
glory and danger alike, and yet not
withstanding go out to meet it.
—Thucydides

Life isn't about how you survive the storm…
but about how you dance in the rain.

Difficulties are meant to rouse, not discourage.
The human spirit is to grow strong by conflict.
—William Ellery Channing